1   What do you want to hear that I haven't told you ?

What do you want to hear that I haven't told you ?
© *Nathanaël AMAH , 2021 NATHAM Collection*

Cover **:** **Fatou**   (with her kind permission)

3   What do you want to hear that I haven't told you ?

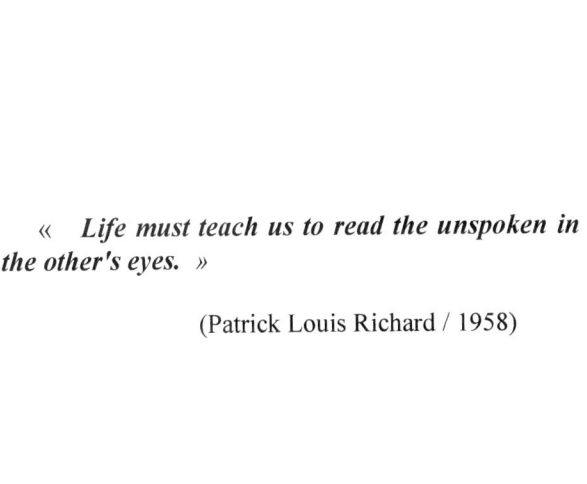

« *Life must teach us to read the unspoken in the other's eyes.* »

(Patrick Louis Richard / 1958)

What do you want to hear that I haven't told you ?

WHAT DO YOU WANT TO HEAR THAT I HAVEN'T TOLD YOU ?

Novel

7   What do you want to hear that I haven't told you ?

8   What do you want to hear that I haven't told you ?

1

In the early afternoon of a gray and rainy autumn day, the horn of a car resounds in front of a building in the street Soufflot, in Paris.

Myriam rushes to the window.

- « *My cab arrived.* » she said calmly.

From the window, she signals to the driver, and asks him to wait.

What do you want to hear that I haven't told you ?

With a nonchalant step as usual, she goes back into the bedroom. A few moments later she returns to the living room, her raincoat and her bag in one hand and in the other, a travel bag containing her first necessities, one or two pairs of pants, two or three sweaters, two pairs of shoes.

Just the bare essentials. She will send for the rest of her things when she has found a place to stay. That's what she promised Arthur.

For the time being, Bintou, her childhood friend, her companion in trouble, has agreed to take her in.

During this morning that preceded the moment when she prepares to say goodbye *(a farewell that will not escape the atmosphere of sadness that usually accompanies separations on a train platform or in the middle of a living room)*, Myriam thought for a long time one last time about her implacable decision to leave.

She wipes away a tear while continuing to

What do you want to hear that I haven't told you ?

sort through her belongings accumulated over the past three years in this apartment where she had made her mark.

She has to clean up. She must leave the place in the state in which she had found it when she arrived in Arthur's life.

For her, there is no other alternative than to leave without looking back.

The main thing is to know how to put on a good face, to keep a certain dignity, a certain prestige. After all, no one is kicking her out. She leaves the place on her own free will.

Therefore, it is no longer possible for her to turn back. What would she look like, she, the woman with the remarkable head bearing, she, the woman with the royal posture ?

She is not acting. She's not telling him: I'm leaving, hold me back.

Too proud to play this game of girlie.

However, she does not ignore what her

What do you want to hear that I haven't told you ?

decision to leave could cost her, in particular, her inevitable return towards a certain precariousness, towards difficult tomorrows knowing that, Arthur proposed to her to reconsider her decision.

One thing is certain: as soon as she crosses the threshold of the apartment's front door, she will find herself alone, even if Bintou will do her best to surround her with her affection.

She will be rescued by her friend, but in what state ?

A state of psychological decay that does not guarantee her the slightest chance of bouncing back in good conditions, even if Bintou's wise advice will help her get back on track without too much damage.

How many, following a deep despair, have taken the step without having succeeded in escaping the vertiginous fall into a black hole with smooth walls that make it impossible to climb back up to the blue sky, and that are capable of disabling the most fierce wills?

What do you want to hear that I haven't told you ?

There is no time for regrets.

When you think about it, how can she dwell on a past that has no future, or no more future ?

Myriam decided to leave a hundred and fifty square meters in the Sorbonne district, for a tiny studio of twenty square meters located in the northern suburbs of Paris.

A regression that was made necessary, in the name of safeguarding her self-esteem.

But never mind the promiscuity.

She has decided to leave, and this is the first time in her short life that she has made such a turn when on the surface everything seemed to be going her way.

Too good to believe, she said to herself in the end.

However, she believed in it for almost three years.

Three years of her life that she now considers totally lost forever.

A real mess.

What do you want to hear that I haven't told you ?

2

 An encounter by chance in the Luxembourg Gardens in Paris.

 She, a nanny in the service of a bourgeois family, walking a baby in a baby carriage.

 He, a professor of classical literature at the Sorbonne, making a detour through the garden before returning to his apartment, on a particularly sunny summer day.

What do you want to hear that I haven't told you ?

A encounter too ordinary to be considered a sign of destiny.

Thousands of people walk through this multifaceted garden every day, which is host to a multitude of sculptures created by illustrious sculptors.

Foreign tourists, Parisians, provincials of all ages.

And among them, that day, Myriam's path crossed that of Arthur.

Generally discreet, Arthur did not resist the urge to say "good evening".

It was just in front of Aimé Millet's sculpture in front of the orangery, on the south side, paying tribute to Phidias.

When she looked up, she saw the face of the man who had just said "Good evening" to her.

Apart from the members of the nanny brigade that she meets daily in this place, and

What do you want to hear that I haven't told you ?

with whom she has a cordial relationship, she had never benefited from the slightest attention from anyone who crossed her path, since she is in charge of this baby.

- « *Good evening Sir* » she said politely.

Arthur smiles broadly.

- « *My name is Arthur, and you ?* »

A few seconds of hesitation later:

- « *Myriam.* »

- « *Nice to meet you! Do you come here often?* »

- « *Yes, sir. Every day.* »

- « *Me, almost every day. I always pass by here to admire this sculpture of Millet. ... By the way, do you know what this sculpture represents?* »

- « *No, Sir.* »

What do you want to hear that I haven't told you ?

Then Arthur began to talk to her about Millet's tribute to the Greek sculptor Phidias, about the beauty of the tribute of a sculptor to another sculptor.

Suddenly, he realizes that his interlocutor who listens to him by politeness, begins to lose patience in front of this flow of passionate, inflamed words.

Not out of disinterest, but because time is running out and she has to go home and give the baby a bath.

This is not a good time to talk about sculpture, especially since for her it's just stones adorning a garden.

- « *I see I'm bothering you.* »

- « *No sir, that's interesting, but I have to get the baby home. I'm late for work. I'm sorry, sir.* »

- « *Okay, I'll leave you to it. Nice to meet you. ... By the way, are you from the neighborhood? Do you go far ?* »

What do you want to hear that I haven't told you ?

- « *Not too much. I work at rue Soufflot.* »

- « *Ah? I live on rue Soufflot.* »

- « *Oh, really !* »

- « *Yes. ... Do you mind if I accompany you?* »

- « *Why not, since we are going to the same place.* » she said coldly.

- « *If it bothers you, I'll go another way. I know the area well.* »

- « *Don't be silly.* »

What do you want to hear that I haven't told you ?

3

 Rue Soufflot.

 Myriam takes leave of her companion of one
evening, by saying to him hardly goodbye,
then disappears behind a door, not reassured
at all.

 She heads straight for the elevator in a panic,
constantly turning back to make sure the
mysterious gentleman in the garden path
didn't have the bad idea to follow her.

What do you want to hear that I haven't told you ?

She presses the elevator button repeatedly, frantically, in a hurry to climb the floors and escape the danger that *(according to her)* lurks around the building.

The baby's bath is quickly done. The baby's snack lasts a long time.

Won over by the nanny's stress, the baby becomes grumpy and refuses to cooperate.

Spoonfuls of applesauce find their mouths closed at their approach, or simply, violently spat out on the nanny's apron.

Myriam is agitated. She becomes irritated, ready to yell at her protégé to make him open his mouth instead of making him want to eat *(as she is accustomed to do)* by pretending to direct the spoon and its contents towards his mouth to indicate that she is going to eat everything. This forces the baby *(worried about losing his food)* to look forward to eating the content of the spoon.
A trick that has always worked well.

What do you want to hear that I haven't told you ?

But this time, she's not in the mood to steal spoonfuls of applesauce.

Her mind is resolutely elsewhere.

Her usual tenderness and meticulousness in her gestures towards the baby seem to have disappeared.

She is eager to finish her shift and go home before nightfall.

Myriam is seized by a certain hysteria. She does not understand what is happening to her.

To walk beside a stranger in the street, is a real novelty for her.

However, the mysterious and erudite stranger did not show the least aggressiveness towards her, quite the contrary.

Was it the fear of not living up to the expectations of this stranger or was it the effect of the overflowing passion of a teacher avid to transmit his knowledge that created

What do you want to hear that I haven't told you ?

this uneasiness in her?

 Perhaps, the feeling of being the victim of a flirt who sought a more or less devious way to approach her, triggered in her an anger that deprived her of her discernment.

 It is true that she always carries in her, the respect of the traditional education which she received in her native village. This education prevents her from letting herself be approached by a stranger in the street, on behalf of safeguarding her precious person, as well as preserving her nudity outside marriage. More serious: to walk next to this stranger in the street, goes against her respectability which could not be tainted with dishonor taking into account the strict application of the precepts of her grandmother who holds them herself from her grandmother.

If we refer to Erving Goffman's thought, the character traits that define her as a woman who is not different from any other woman, even if she conceives and sees herself as a woman apart.

As the daughter of a traditional chief, she has become a nanny by force of circumstance.

This is not so different from what happens in the village where all the children are collectively looked after and educated by the community of women.

Therefore, being a nanny does not go against her principles, even if, here in Paris, with regard to the baby she is in charge of, she is in the role of a substitute mother, with overwhelming responsibilities on her shoulders.

Therefore, her social position does not disqualify her from this teacher, the depositary of knowledge.

The problem that appears in this unlikely relationship is not a supposed gap between knowledge and non-knowledge, but between the spontaneity of the one who comes up against the mistrust of the other.

The good faith of the teacher did not find a favorable echo in the face of Myriam's suspicion.

Then, there would not exist in any way, the slightest point of intersection between the ignorance of the fact of having aroused mistrust and this real mistrust which inhabits Myriam, making vain all the thoughts which would militate in favor of a hypothetical bringing together.

What do you want to hear that I haven't told you ?

4

Arthur, goes back up the street and returns home happy with his day.

He ignores all this mistrust that he aroused in Myriam, the lady with the baby carriage.

Once he gets rid of his shoes and work clothes, he indulges as usual in his favorite ritual: three or four slices of sausage on a plate, bread, pickles, a glass of apple cider, his CD of Mozart's clarinet concerto K. 622, which he listens to religiously while enjoying his snack, beating the measure with his feet

What do you want to hear that I haven't told you ?

under the table.

This is his time to relax and nothing can upset him.

Afterwards, he has to correct student's homework and prepare for the next day's classes until dinner time.

His encounter with Myriam in this garden did not make much of an impression on him.

He had already done the same thing with tourists passing through Paris, visiting the Luxembourg garden, without remembering every face he met.

Yet, as he went to bed, reviewing his day, his mind suddenly went to the face of the person to whom, a few hours earlier, he had explained Millet's sculpture paying tribute to the Greek sculptor Phidias.

He remembered her bright face, but was intrigued by the sadness in her eyes.

She seemed to be putting on a good face

What do you want to hear that I haven't told you ?

while being absorbed in her thoughts.

 The impression he had from that brief encounter, during which he had played tour guide, came to the surface.

 He put his head on his pillow with this strange idea that he would like to see her again.

 See her again for what?

 Perhaps to apologize for having bothered her during her walk with the baby she looks after.

 Indeed, his propensity to think of himself as an indispensable person, leads him to consider himself as a person that everyone needs to cultivate.

 For him, it doesn't matter where: in a classroom, or in the great amphitheater of life that is the streets, gardens, parks, etc., the important thing is to manage to transmit knowledge.

 This professional deformation sometimes

leads him to situations like the one that placed him in front of Myriam, for whom his desire to transmit his knowledge was the strongest.

Generally, it is afterwards that he realizes the consequences of his intrusion in the lives of people who, in fact, are not in demand of anything.

At the Sorbonne, he is Mr. Arthur Païchet, professor emeritus, respected by all.

In the Luxembourg garden, he is an ordinary individual whose importance is equal to that of all those he meets.

But his desire to transmit his knowledge always comes back at a gallop.

Deep down, he no longer likes the world around him and in which he lives. He is sorry to see all that part of the population that indulges in an intellectual inertia that keeps it in an ignorance of which it is not even aware.

His way of remedying this "intellectual catastrophe" *(as he puts it)* is to transmit

What do you want to hear that I haven't told you ?

knowledge whenever he has the opportunity.

He has always dreamed of living in London so that he could speak at Speakers Corner in Hyde Park, a mecca for free speech.

For him, such a space would be the ideal place to "sow knowledge".

But the Sorbonne is another place of excellence in the transmission of knowledge.

What do you want to hear that I haven't told you ?

5

If this is his nature, how is it that two women, *(who shared his life successively)*, left him after a few years of common life?

Among the reasons commonly mentioned: lack of communication, boredom.

How can one be bored with a person who is constantly thirsting for communication?

Apparently, he could sit for long hours

What do you want to hear that I haven't told you ?

without opening his mouth, as if he did not live in his body, as if his surroundings were completely non-existent, even transparent, creating a void, an unbearable atmosphere.

Paradoxical isn't it?

He, the voluble one, the communicator, the knowing one, the one who seduces his audience, the darling of the amphitheaters, the one who approaches the strangers to deliver his knowledge.

Isn't it the worst criticism one can make of him if he is indeed Mr. Arthur P by qualifying him as an unsociable person according to the allegations of his two ex-wives?

Two distinct testimonies which corroborate the same description of this man whom they married after having been impressed by his eloquence, seduced by his delicacy.

Presumably, it is the same person, the one who is on the outside this brilliant spirit and who becomes at home this pale image of the ideal husband.

What do you want to hear that I haven't told you ?

For him who changes his personality once he gets home, is it his true nature that takes over?

What about his attitude outside?

A role of composition?

An actor mastering his role to perfection in front of an audience already won over?

According to Gilbert CESBRON: "***People without personality play a character***".

What to believe?

We have all been confronted at some point in our lives with a downturn, a bout of fatigue, a weariness, making us silent, absent, distant. However, this does not make us unsociable people, people devoid of any personality.

The other question we have the right to ask ourselves is: Is Arthur, despite everything, a happy man in his life?

Unless he is true to his true nature, he cannot

What do you want to hear that I haven't told you ?

be happy, torn between the man he is at home and the one his fame requires him to show, once he is out of the house.

Appearances versus personality.

How to balance these two notions knowing that, nowadays, the weight put on the appearances is preponderant compared to the need to assert our personality?

Seen from the outside, Arthur's double personality seems both complementary and contradictory.

Complementary in the sense that he needs this notoriety which gives him the illusion of greatness outside to compensate for his almost non-existence at home.

Contradictory because his life at home is synonymous with solitude which resists the benefits of a feminine presence, source of inspiration and joy of living.

He carries this feeling of loneliness in himself as well as carrying a cross all his life.

The presence of his ex-wives at his side, did not make the weight in the face of his deep desire to be alone.

So what is this idea of having introduced at home a foreign presence that has only exacerbated the development and affirmation of this unbearable character, which makes him unlivable, even repulsive?

Why this need to live together since his deep desire is to be alone?

What do you want to hear that I haven't told you ?

6

Myriam returned to work the next day with fear in her stomach, despite the advice of her friend Bintou to whom she told through the menu, what happened to her, advice that failed to tranquilize her.

Yet, according to her friend, this may be the sign of fate. The opportunity to take shelter and secure a bright future, to end with the galleys, to draw a line on her past life.

What do you want to hear that I haven't told you ?
© *Nathanaël AMAH , 2021 NATHAM Collection*

According to this friend who wishes her well, Myriam should provoke a new encounter and try to seduce the gentleman.

This is not at all to the taste of Myriam who does not see herself in the posture of a woman at a discount who seeks to settle down at all costs.

Myriam's life was anything but a fairy tale.

From an arranged marriage from which she escaped, saved by a benevolent cousin *(but secretly in love with her)*, the boss of an import-export establishment in Milan, Italy.

Highly respected by the diaspora and well established in business circles, he manages to obtain a visa to allow Myriam to join him in Italy.

Myriam's arrival in Italy was the start of a series of setbacks.

Promises for a better future turned from the start into a series of disappointments :

What do you want to hear that I haven't told you ?

repeated rapes, a job as subordinate, a life almost in prison, not allowing her the slightest spiritual and physical development.

Result: a predictable pregnancy, followed by a difficult delivery in psychologically deplorable conditions.

The bad surprises follow one another around her.

Her three-year-old daughter *(a beautiful doe-eyed doll)* is taken away from her without notice and sent to the country overnight to be educated in the pure family tradition.

Depressed, Myriam is at the end of her rope.

She would like to return to her country to her daughter, whom she dreams about every night, but the benevolent cousin had confiscated her passport and all the documents allowing her to travel in and out of Italy.

She only knows a few words in Italian, allowing her to go shopping in the

What do you want to hear that I haven't told you ?

neighborhood.

There were very few familiar faces in her immediate environment.
But at the bakery, she eventually made friends with one of the saleswomen who managed to communicate with her.

Since the benevolent cousin demands fresh bread every day, Myriam got into the habit of going to the bakery every morning.

This chore is no longer a chore.

Thus, the pleasure of seeing her new friend every morning, except on her day of rest *(she herself is obliged to go to her mother's house to whom she has entrusted the custody of her son)*, has gradually given her back the taste for life.

Thanks to her, and in the greatest secrecy, she managed to learn Italian, which she speaks with a hint of a village accent. It doesn't matter.

This was an essential step in the reconquest

What do you want to hear that I haven't told you ?

of her freedom, because she had decided to reconquer her freedom.

She could not bring herself to end her life in slavery.

Knowing the language of a country is the most important thing to "live" in that country.

For the benevolent cousin, keeping Myriam in complete ignorance of the habits and customs of Italy was a guarantee that she would not try to escape.

He had promised her many things, including learning the language and eventually resuming her studies to acquire a serious profession for her future, and especially to become a free woman, free to make her own choices in life.

Yes ! … free to make her own choices in life.

7

To put his distrust to sleep and make him believe that she remained the village girl of the first days, freshly arrived in Italy, Myriam continued to endure his assaults each time his wife went to the family business, him making only a brief appearance during the day.

To satisfy the sexual desires of the benevolent cousin, the scenario always unfolded in the same way.

What do you want to hear that I haven't told you ?

As soon as the legitimate wife left, at the very second, the master's voice rang out from the conjugal room:

"Myriam ! "

She understood from then on the meaning of this call.

She knew that she would have to undergo once again the assaults of this repulsive individual whom she called "uncle".

On the bed, fists clenched to contain her anger and avoid committing the irreparable by tearing him to pieces, eyes closed not to see that hideous face and those lustful eyes very close to her face, lips clenched to prevent that pasty tongue coming out of a smelly mouth from entering her mouth, striving to breathe every other time not to smell the fetid breath emanating from the unwashed mouth of this unscrupulous uncle, the fat pig who tramples with his foot the oath made to the family back home, and finally, moved by this irrepressible desire to recover her freedom by sacrificing herself, she gives him access to her intimacy

What do you want to hear that I haven't told you ?

with tears in her eyes.

After which, he ordered her to put the room in order to erase the traces of his crime while the gentleman went to bask in his bathtub whistling, totally satisfied with his beginning of morning.

The increasingly strong friendship which binds Myriam to the saleswoman made it possible, with the wire of time, to start her emancipation.

Thus, she knew the way not to fall pregnant any more thanks to the use of the contraceptive pill of last generation.

This allowed her to be protected from an unwanted pregnancy, as her uncle stubbornly refused to use a condom, on behalf of tradition, despite the pleas of his slave.

She was thus able to escape the consequences of a new childbirth, synonymous with a new heartbreak.

Aware of the fact that, seen from the outside,

What do you want to hear that I haven't told you ?

her attitude can be assimilated to a form of prostitution *(sex for food)*, in spite of everything, she consoles herself by convincing herself that for her, it is the price of her freedom.

Sacrificing herself to regain her freedom is the ultimate gesture to alleviate her despair.

To justify herself *(as if it were necessary)*, she evokes the analogy between her behavior and that of a wild beast caught in the jaws of a wolf trap that self-mutilates to regain its freedom and escape death.

In doing so, her goal is not to escape death, but to succeed in getting her hands on her papers abusively held by her uncle, a crucial step towards her freedom.

What ends up happening by a curious chance.

Indeed, one day, while cleaning the room, she discovered the bag containing the important papers, placed on the bedside table, while her uncle was lounging in his bath once his crime was done.

Machinally, while watching her back, she opened the bag and discovered among the papers, her passport and her residence permit.

Like a microprocessor, her brain went into "rapid analysis" mode, beating all speed records:

- should she take her papers and run away right away?

- Should she wait for the next opportunity to better prepare her escape while not knowing when that bag will resurface on the bedside table?

She is hot. She is overexcited. She wants to shout her joy to the world. But the bathroom is down the hall.

In front of the bag, her papers in the hands, Myriam shakes of all her being. She does not know what to do. She reviews all the scenarios, going from the opportunity to run away right away, to the murder of the uncle in his bathtub with a pair of scissors.

What do you want to hear that I haven't told you ?

But, she ends up choosing the most reasonable solution but also the most risky from her point of view, namely, to withdraw and hide her papers while continuing her life with this uncle as if everything was normal in order to better prepare her escape.

Then, quickly, she goes out of the room and hides her precious documents in her suitcase and returns to finish her work in the bedroom.

What do you want to hear that I haven't told you ?

8

The day went on without a hitch.

No summons to the Gestapo to find out where the papers had gone.

Indeed, back from the bathroom, the uncle, without inventorying the contents of the bag, put it back in its usual place and locked it in the cupboard, the key of which he never leaves.

What do you want to hear that I haven't told you ?

Despite the calm that reigned all day, Myriam had a very bad night.

Her anguish is real. She is divided between the joy of having found her papers, and the apprehension to see her uncle bursting into her room shouting in search of the papers which would have disappeared from the bag.

Too risky to keep the papers in the only place where the furious uncle would go without hesitation.

What to do?

She thought to herself that night would bring advice.

She ended up falling asleep in the middle of the night, half of her in the arms of Morpheus, the other half sitting on a chair, standing guard over her suitcase.

Clearly, a night in dots.

The next morning, in a state of extreme tiredness having cogitated part of the night, she prepared to go to the bakery.

Machinally, she took her papers, placed them in an envelope and slipped it into the pocket of her raincoat.

When she arrived at the bakery, she stood in line like everyone else.

When it was her turn, she asked for three Ciabatta breads as usual. She then went to the cash register held by the owner.

But as she passed her friend, she nodded to her. Sandra knew something was wrong, given the tired face of her friend. She had never seen her in such a tired state.

So Sandra anticipated her break and went to join her outside the bakery.

Myriam burst into tears as she handed her the envelope, adding:

- « *Sandra, I trust you with my life. Can you please keep this for me.* »

What do you want to hear that I haven't told you ?

Sandra is taken aback. She hesitates to take the envelope not knowing what it contains.

- « *Myriam what is it? What is happening? Please tell me.* »

- « *These are my papers that my cousin had hidden since my arrival. I just found them. I have to leave this house. I can't take it anymore. ... Please help me.* »

Sandra stared at her for a brief moment, then agreed to take the envelope, adding:

- « *Myriam, I trust you. Do not make trouble for me. Don't you?* »

- « *No No No! ... Don't worry. I'll explain later. I thank you very much. You are a life saver. Thank you, thank you, thank you!* »

Sandra pushed aside her blouse slightly, put the envelope and its contents in one of the pockets of her pants, and went back to work.

Myriam did the same, with a lighter heart.

What do you want to hear that I haven't told you ?

At least she thought, her uncle would not be able to get his hands on her papers and thwart her escape plan.

A few weeks later, after many adventures, against all odds, Myriam arrived in Paris, welcomed by Bintou, her childhood friend.

The priority of priorities: finding a job.

What can she do?

Not much, apart from taking care of the cleanliness of her benevolent uncle's apartment and, incidentally, ensuring his good morning mood once or twice a week.

Considering this persistent feeling of almost sickly lack that she feels since her little girl was taken away from her, the only job that could allow her to fill this void left by her daughter sent to the country, and to make her anxieties disappear, would consist in making her gravitate around a job putting her in the presence of children and in relation with their education.

What do you want to hear that I haven't told you ?

She will be able to "play" the surrogate mother while earning a living.

Myriam chose to prospect for a job as a nanny.

This is how she landed on rue Soufflot in a bourgeois family who did not hesitate to hire her, because of her calmness, her good manners, and moreover because she spoke Italian, the mistress of the house being of Italian origin herself.

What do you want to hear that I haven't told you ?

9

 "***It is perhaps a sign of the destiny***" had said to her Bintou.

 Despite her avowed dislike for all the uncles of the earth, indeed of the whole universe, this little sentence resounds in all her being with a particular echo.

 However, she does everything to get rid of it while trying to concentrate on her work.

What do you want to hear that I haven't told you ?

Calm is finally back.

The program of the morning: to make two or three food races in the nearby supermarket while the baby will leave at the pediatrician with his mom.

Then, while waiting for the baby to return, a small ironing session. An activity that reminds her of her past life. But now, she is paid to do it. It's more acceptable to her.

Middle of the afternoon.

Time for the daily walk.

Myriam lingers in front of the mirror hung in the entrance.

The baby is impatient in his mother's arms.

Finally:

- "*Andiamo!* "

Jeremy holds out his arms to her. She picks him up and hugs him tightly.

What do you want to hear that I haven't told you ?
© *Nathanaël AMAH , 2021 NATHAM Collection*

Martine doesn't understand. Since Myriam has been at her service, this is the first time she has observed such behavior. She is worried a bit :

- "***Tutto bene, Myriam?*** "

- "***Si, signora***. "

Rue Soufflot.

Myriam takes the direction of the garden of Luxembourg.

Clear way. Moderate speed. Senses on alert.

For the moment, all is well.

The Luxembourg garden in sight.

The usual circuit. Once, twice, three times.

Nothing to report.

No crowd in front of a self-proclaimed guide.

What do you want to hear that I haven't told you ?
© *Nathanaël AMAH , 2021 NATHAM Collection*

No need to wait any longer.

Return to the apartment.

Rue Soufflot, higher.

Day of rest.

Arthur as a well organized bachelor, proceeds to the cleaning of his apartment. At the end of the morning, shopping at the supermarket. Ordinary activities of a day of rest.

10

Days go by.

Nothing to report.

Normal life in this middle-class neighborhood.

Then one day, while going to the supermarket, Myriam came face to face with Arthur who was leaving his apartment to go to the Sorbonne.

What do you want to hear that I haven't told you ?

Arthur, carrying his yellow schoolbag, stopped in front of her.

- "*Hello.* "

Myriam recognized him.

- "*Good morning, sir.* "

- "*Do you remember me? We met in front of Millet's sculpture in the Luxembourg Gardens*. "

- "*Yes, I remember.* "

- "*I wanted to see you again to apologize.* "

- "*Why?*"

- "*For having inconvenienced you by approaching you as I did.* "

- "*That's all right, sir*. "

- "*Please stop calling me sir, my name is Arthur. And you?*"

What do you want to hear that I haven't told you ?

- "*Myriam.* "

- "*Nice to meet you! Where are you going? Aren't you working today?* "

- *Yes, I'm working. I'm going to do some shopping at the supermarket.* "

- "*Okay! I'm going to give my classes at the Sorbonne.* "

- "*Okay! I wish you a good day.* "

- *Thank you Myriam. To you too.* "

But at the time of leaving, moved by a sudden desire, Arthur dared to propose to see her again.

- *Myriam I live here on the second floor. Come by one day for a cup of tea if you feel like it. It will be my pleasure to discuss with you.* "

Myriam hesitates for a moment and then:

What do you want to hear that I haven't told you ?

- "*Maybe I'll drop by, one of these days.* "

- " *So, see you very soon.* "

Myriam walked away.

In the evening, back home, Myriam told Bintou in great detail about her second encounter with the professor.

Bintou exclaimed, raising her arm to the sky:

- "*My sister, I told you, it is the sign of destiny....Go have tea and breakfast at the same time. If he offers you dinner too, accept! If he offers you to make a baby with him, accept! Accept everything! Do you understand?* "

- "*Bintou, you are really sick! He just offered me a cup of tea. Nothing else.* "

- "*Yes we know where the cup of tea starts and where it ends.* "

- "*Don't be silly!* "

What do you want to hear that I haven't told you ?
© *Nathanaël AMAH , 2021 NATHAM Collection*

- "*Seriously, promise me you'll go see him.* "

- "*To tell you the truth, I don't know yet, I'll think about it.* "

- "*Think fast and hard sister, don't let your chance go to waste.* "

What do you want to hear that I haven't told you ?

11

A week passed.

Bintou continued her harassment without getting tired.

Myriam still does not decide.

Her trauma is still alive. She cannot forget her fear of men.

Barely out of the clutches of the hell that was her life, blinded by her hatred for all the beings who have a penis between the legs, and

What do you want to hear that I haven't told you ?

still feeling the stigmata of these years of suffering in her flesh, she does not manage to make the mourning of this horrible past, which does not allow her *(in any case)* to make the difference between the predators who massacred her youth and the good intentions of Arthur who seems to be the track to be explored with *(of course)* a thousand and one precautions.

She wonders how she could behave in front of a man who desires her, animated by a *(visibly)* sincere love?

How to deliver her body so that hands deemed "inappropriate" can touch it?

How to manage to unclench her thighs in front of a man coming from nowhere without showing this self-protective repulsion?

How does she recognize a sincere man among the multitude?

What is a sincere man? She asks herself.

Is it the one who comes with good intentions

What do you want to hear that I haven't told you ?

and promises on his lips?

The one who presents himself with all his imperfections, his roughness, his bad temper and who makes the loved one understand that everything can be improved?

Or the one that remains, even when the desire has evaporated, like a perfume bottle that over time has let its fragrance escape while remaining in a good place on the dressing table?

How do we know if under the shell, there is a magnificent heart, ready to beat even harder to absorb the overflow of love that we can show it?

A Sufi proverb teaches us this:

"*Sincerity is the pearl that forms in the shell of the heart.* "

So, let's imagine the slow process that allows the formation of the pearl.

At the beginning, how many shells, and at the

end, how many pearls?

Big sigh.

Bintou is desperate in front of all this questioning which undermines her attempt to make her friend Myriam yield so that she can taste in her turn before dying, the flesh of this so particular fruit, with the sweet and addictive savour which is happiness.

For her, this questioning has no reason to be. It is a question of seizing the hand that fate is holding out to her.

But isn't the devil's hand *(with dirty and hooked nails)* often gloved? Immaculate gloves, magnificent, with an incredibly silky touch.

She seems to forget this detail.

She doesn't care about these diabolical considerations. Devil or not devil, what matters for her is this cup of tea which desperately waits for her friend, rue Soufflot.

What do you want to hear that I haven't told you ?

12

 Harassed by the daily supplications of Bintou, Myriam took the decision to honor with her presence, the invitation proposed by Arthur.

 This can only happen on a day of rest, a Saturday or a Sunday.

 Why ?

What do you want to hear that I haven't told you ?

It is like that!

Bintou is relieved.

Now, how to get dressed?

Pants for safety?

A dress, but which one for the tea party not at the Queen of England's palace, but on rue Soufflot at Arthur's?

New animated evenings at Bintou's who opted for the dress.

They have a week to decide. Discussions are going well. Fitting sessions punctuated the evenings.

And one evening, finally they both agree on the dress, but not for the same reasons: for Myriam, it is not too short, it covers well her knees. For Bintou, it is very tight, bringing out her forms, which is essential for the objective to reach.

She strides with joy. She has almost

What do you want to hear that I haven't told you ?

succeeded.

She proposes to style her hair.

An Afro Puff for example *(hairstyle which consists in attaching the Afro hair in order to have a voluminous cabbage)*, would put her face in value.

Myriam accepted the proposal without discussion.

A first appointment must be decisive, Bintou keeps harping on.

An argument which ends up finding a favorable echo at Myriam.

But she doesn't give up: it is only an invitation to have tea.

She does not want to sacrifice herself to satisfy the whims of Bintou, who thinks she is a "matchmaker", just like in her country since the announcement of the invitation.

She does not resent her. She even finds her

touching, she who failed in her relationship not so long ago.

She doesn't blame her insofar as she cares about her happiness. Finally a person who wants her well after all these years.

However, she would not want to be her puppet that she would manipulate as she pleased under the guise of seeking her happiness.

What do you want to hear that I haven't told you ?

13

Saturday, 4 pm precisely, rue Soufflot.

A cab has just parked.

On board, Myriam, dressed like a wedding day, pays the fare and gets out of the car, leaving behind, the scent of a very expensive perfume.

She rings the intercom. The door is unlocked. She enters the building, and goes up to the second floor.

What do you want to hear that I haven't told you ?
© *Nathanaël AMAH , 2021 NATHAM Collection*

While waiting for the arrival of the elevator, Arthur leaves the apartment and stands in front of his door.

Arrival of the elevator.

The door opens.

Myriam appears in all her splendor and advances towards him.

Arthur does not believe his eyes.

The bright beauty of his guest in perfect agreement with her dress and her hairstyle *(bravo Bintou)*, leaves him without voice.

He stares at her for a long time. Myriam is almost embarrassed.

Then:

- "**Hello Myriam.** "

- **Hello Arthur.** "

What do you want to hear that I haven't told you ?

- "*Welcome.* "

- " *Thank you.* "

- " *You are splendid.* "

Myriam sketches a smile which emphasizes her dimples that Arthur had not noticed until then.

Arthur invites her to enter the apartment first.

Myriam executes the request without hurrying too much. What gave the opportunity to Arthur to observe her from the back. He is subjugated by so much beauty.

Arthur closes the door and joins her at the end of the corridor which leads to the lounge.

As a well-mannered host, Arthur proposes to her to visit the places.

Myriam accepts.

Bintou would have wanted to be a small ant to hide in a corner of the apartment and to

What do you want to hear that I haven't told you ?

observe what occurs there, even if Myriam promised to tell her everything. She is persuaded not to see Myriam again so soon. She only knows why.

Precision : she insisted a lot that Myriam wears pearls around the waist under her dress. Once again, only she knows why.

For the "neophytes", it is the final touch not to neglect for a successful date.

Although Myriam agreed to adorn herself with these pearls, she keeps nevertheless in her, this reserve, this quasi coldness which would discourage the most courageous, the most enterprising courtiers.

In the apartment, Arthur had done things well: tea, pastry and Mozart *(his final touch)*.

Between two compliments, going from one thing to another, Arthur could not help but display his culture. Everything goes through it: the tea ceremony in Japan, using learned terms such as chanoyu, sado, or chado, the link between this traditional art inspired in part by Buddhism, ... , the composition of the cake served, gluten free cake, the damage caused by gluten, the structure of Mozart's concerti.

During this moment of sharing tea, which by definition should be synonymous with suspended time, a moment during which silence is golden, Arthur occupied the entire sound space without interruption, transforming his living room into an amphitheater.

Myriam put on a good show throughout this afternoon of general culture.

What do you want to hear that I haven't told you ?

14

Back home around six o'clock, Bintou rushed in:

- "*Well, tell me!* "

- "*There is nothing to tell you*." Myriam answers while undressing.

- "*Are you joking?* "

- "*No*!"

What do you want to hear that I haven't told you ?

- "*You went to do what then?*"

- "*To have tea.*"

- "*So?*"

- "*We had tea....Bintou, please let me breathe.*"

- "*And that's all?*"

- "*Yes!*"

- "*Reassure me, you will see each other again?*"

- "*Yes, I heard.*"

- "*When?*"

- "*Next week.*"

- "*Still for tea?*"

- "*No, for lunch.*"

- "*Sister, refuse the restaurant, you have to*

What do you want to hear that I haven't told you ?
© *Nathanaël AMAH , 2021 NATHAM Collection*

have lunch at his place. Do you want me to make you lunch to take there? "

Myriam smiles.

- *"**Bintou, do you think you are in the village?** "*

- *"**Village or no village, you have to get there, sister.**"*

- *"**Bintou, you really have no morality.** "*

- ***Who is talking to you about morality? Do you think this is the time to talk about morality? You have to get back what the sky sent you. That's all we ask. Sister, don't disappoint me. Okay?***"

Myriam bursts out laughing, and doesn't stop laughing.

- *"**Bintou! Listen to me: the sky has not sent me anything and there is nothing to recover.** "*

- *"**Seriously, do you want me to make you***

What do you want to hear that I haven't told you ?

something for your lunch with him next Sunday? "

- "No, that's not happening.......How would I look? Do you see me showing up at his apartment with my pot? ... Do you ever stop? "

- No, as long as the case is not in the bag. You can believe me. "

Myriam let out a big sigh.

What do you want to hear that I haven't told you ?

15

 Two or three lunches later, the good understanding between Myriam and Arthur had turned into a desire to see each other more often.

 Bintou's wise advice began to have an effect.

 Next step, according to her, Myriam must go to live with Arthur.

 - " ***You don't think about it for a moment. I***

What do you want to hear that I haven't told you ?

am not a girl to be fixed up. I am not one of the unsold items left on the market stalls to be sold at the end of the market. If Arthur doesn't ask me, I will never allow myself to go and settle in his apartment with him. Such behavior would do me wrong rather than do me any good in this relationship that I am beginning to enjoy. "

- "You call this a relationship? You see each other from time to time, you look each other in the white of the eye and you go home. You call that a relationship?... Tell me Myriam, did he try to kiss you? Tell me honestly. "

- "No. Why are you asking me that? "

- "No? He's never tried to kiss you with everything you put in his sight? He doesn't want your lips? No ? Ah, that's what I was saying. What is this relationship that is wasting your time? "

- "Bintou, it's just a friendship. It's nothing more than that. Can you understand that? "

What do you want to hear that I haven't told you ?

- "Friendship! Friendship! Give me a break, sister. Don't you think it's high time you take your revenge on life ? "

- "Revenge on what? Why should it be on him? What did he do to deserve this? Because he hasn't kissed me yet? Perhaps he will when the time will come, and if, as you have often told me, he embodies that sign which fate has sent me. ... He is an extremely kind gentleman to me. He is very cultured. He's teaching me things that I didn't even know about. "

- "Okay! If you want to learn new things, then maybe it would be better if you return back to school. Don't disappoint me sister. I'm telling you for the last time. "

After these words, Bintou went to bed.

Myriam remained alone for a moment and then went to bed in her turn.

As usual, the words hammered by her friend Bintou, continue to resonate in her mind.

What do you want to hear that I haven't told you ?

And if she was right?

She is aware that there is a good understanding between them, but perhaps, this sign of the destiny really needs a small blow of inch as Bintou suggests it?

Nothing is less sure.

It doesn't matter where she lives, but for her, tradition forbids such a step. She cannot go and provoke a union with a man she barely knows.

Man desires woman. Man deserves woman.

Yes, but with such blinders on, she won't get very far and will only fail in her quest for happiness, at least by not following the good recommendations of her friend Bintou who seems to understand the situation better from her outside position.

Indeed, from her observation post, and taking into account the painful past of her friend, Bintou is able to pilot the events. Her dearest desire, to give back the thrill to her friend.

What do you want to hear that I haven't told you ?

16

The idea made its way.

Myriam seemed more relaxed, more open, more provocative.

Arthur noticed the metamorphosis.

Myriam no longer walks beside him like a person walking with another person.

From now on, she takes his arm during their walks through Paris.

What do you want to hear that I haven't told you ?

From then on, he could dare a certain approach to win his friend's heart.

Thus, he invited her to a restaurant one evening to announce his desire to propose her to live with him.

As a dignified woman and respectful of tradition, she reserved her answer until the next day. This earned her the disapproval of her friend Bintou who reproached her, her excessive modesty.

The next day, the answer was yes. A definitive yes.

Then, for the first time, Arthur undertook to kiss her.

She agreed to get closer to him by looking at him fixedly in the eyes.

She let herself be kissed.

She made him the same.

What do you want to hear that I haven't told you ?

She received this first kiss with a lot of emotions, the first in her life as a free woman.

For the first time she could decide who could touch her. She was able to taste the flavor that she had forbidden herself all these years.

This first step was reported in great detail to Bintou, the big-hearted coach, who had been dissatisfied with the slow pace of events.

If it were up to her, a baby would already be on his way. The baby of happiness that will not replace the one that was sent back home, but that will be the testimony of happiness found, no matter his color.

By her nature, in the clutches of the devil or in the arms of a gentleman, Myriam does not know how to give herself.

Some would say that she is not a clever and active woman.

She is not the kind of woman who would behave lightly in the secret of the bedroom. She is a reserved woman who would suffer rather than lead the events.

She doesn't know how to say: do this, do that.

This is her deep nature, and her painful past has not helped.

So, without being asked, Coach Bintou gave her a few recipes of her own to help her turn a cold heart into a sulphurous volcano, spitting flames.

This had the effect of making her laugh, not seeing herself in the skin of a seductress.

Not having any reference in the matter, her image of the couple is to be invented.

But, is Arthur the right partner to accompany this resurection?

What could this twice-married character, who never wanted to have children, who is centered on his own person, bring to her?

These parameters totally escaped the analysis of Bintou who literally pushed her into the arms of Arthur.

Crucial parameters which will determine the future of this couple which has hardly been born.

Myriam ignores all of her real faculties to determine herself. She ignores her potential to become the woman dreamed for Arthur. She probably doesn't need the authority and the support of a man to settle down in the western sense of the word.

She will have to learn all the codes and to know how to decode them, in front of Arthur, in the real life with Arthur.

The same goes for Arthur who, for the first time, is confronted with another civilization than his own, through a new woman in his life.

All his bookish knowledge will be of no use to him in front of the reality of the life, in the presence of Myriam who comes to him, with a scarred and damaged soul.

What do you want to hear that I haven't told you ?

When Arthur said to her that evening:

 "***Do you want to live with me?***"

what did he mean?

 What does this question mean on either side of the same river that flows between them?

 For Arthur, it could mean:

 "Stay with me, let's enjoy life together, let's be happy. "

 For her:

 "Okay, I'm coming but take care of me, make me happy. "

 For Bintou, in the middle of this river making the subtle connection between them both:

 "Come, settle down, give me kids as much as you can. "

 Not simple!

What do you want to hear that I haven't told you ?

But to simplify, could we apply to their budding couple, the precept of Nelly Alard, namely:

"***The husband makes the couple, the wife makes the family.*** "

Big question.

What do you want to hear that I haven't told you ?

17

The first months of her new life were beyond her expectations.

A real enchantment, the discovery of life as a couple by mutual consent. Learning the art of taming the other, the pleasure of living in the undisguised hope of perpetual bliss, the confirmation that carnal relations are not synonymous with suffering and degradation.

Myriam applies herself day after day to

become, to incarnate the woman who gives and receives.

This *(seen from the shore of tradition)* is a surprising novelty for her, traditionally used to giving without receiving anything in return.

She became aware of the need to reconcile tradition with the realities of her life with Arthur.

It was not always easy for her, sometimes forced to make the big gap to avoid the rupture.

And who says rupture, says disagreement, which implies to keep a certain distance allowing to analyze coldly what could *(under the prism of the relation man / woman, or from a civilization point of view)* sow the discord within the couple.

On his side, Arthur had no other choice than to conform to the requirements conveyed by the image of the man in a couple relationship, namely: the one who reassures, the one who supports, the one who is the pillar.

It seems that the joy of being together in the evening *(she, in her role of the loving and caring woman, he, the pillar on whom she can lean and confide her preoccupations)*, has been the cement of their couple, apart from all other considerations.

Myriam seems happy, but on the other hand, she is constantly in demand to the great surprise of Arthur: in emotional demand, in communicational demand, in sexual demand.

On the other hand, for Arthur who, in his clothes of communicator, haloed by his displayed dynamism, by his natural charm, everything concurs to guarantee the success of this challenge.

But, little by little the projects of life *(marriage, children, voyages)* federative at the beginning of the relation, are constantly postponed to later without a valid reason.

"***We'll see.*** "

The usual sentence heard at each recall of

What do you want to hear that I haven't told you ?

Myriam whose intention is to substitute her companion *(called to other tasks)* in order to relieve him of the organization of these events that are discussed and that are important to her heart.

Tirelessly, Myriam puts back in the center of the couple these projects of life *(essential for her, essential for the survival of her couple)* so that they are not thrown to the oblivion.

vain attempts.

She turns a deaf ear to the injunctions of Bintou to get pregnant in secret, so called to put Arthur in the corner, but by her nature, and by considering that a child is made by two persons, she cannot oblige herself to such a maneuver which would discredit her automatically and would worsen the fragility which starts to appear within her couple.

Months have passed.

The couple is at the beginning of its second year.

What do you want to hear that I haven't told you ?
© *Nathanaël AMAH , 2021 NATHAM Collection*

Nothing moves. The days pass and are all alike.

Arthur begins to drag his feet when it is time to go home. He could no longer bear the constant pressure that he could see in the eyes of his partner, who for her part, was becoming more and more silent, which did not bode well.

A silence announcing a powerful and devastating storm.

Myriam wants to avoid at all costs to arrive there. She invested herself too much in this relation to fail so near a goal whose contours are more and more blurred.

What do you want to hear that I haven't told you ?

18

Bintou does not give up.

Feeling that the situation was getting out of hand on the one hand, and to prevent it from getting totally out of control on the other hand, she studied all the options and multiplied her advice to help her friend get out of it.

The inventory of measures she recommends

What do you want to hear that I haven't told you ?

includes various actions such as: prayer sessions in church, fasting days to invoke the patron saint of desperate causes, and if that is not enough, recourse to the exorcist in her country.

Myriam thinks that no intervention (even if it is divine) can replace the good old dialogue which allows to calm the tensions and to rebuild the cracked building.

Yes, Bintou retorts, provided that her dear "brother-in-law" *(as she calls him)*, is willing to listen and dialogue. She does not understand why Myriam does not put him against the wall and force him to marry her.

In their country as she says, there would have been a delegation of village elders who would have made the trip to try to reason with the recalcitrant fiancé.

But there is no fiancé, she is not in their country, let alone the village.

She doesn't seem to know what life is like in the West, where everything is a matter of consensus, where nothing is obtained by force or arbitrarily.

People marry freely and divorce freely.

There is no substitute for the sacrosanct principle of individual freedom.

Myriam has understood this and cannot therefore comply with the multiple injunctions of her friend.

At the most, in her inner dialogue with her creator, she could surreptitiously slip in a little supplication to ask for his help. That's all she would accept to do in front of her friend's despair.

Seen from the outside, Myriam does not seem to be affected too much by the situation within her couple. She is surprised herself, surprised to see herself so confident given the inevitable breakdown of her relationship.

Beginning of the third year of life together.

The balance sheet: not very glorious.

What do you want to hear that I haven't told you ?
© *Nathanaël AMAH , 2021 NATHAM Collection*

Sometimes a glimmer of hope, sometimes complete despair.

Bintou gives up and stays away from this affair. She is disappointed by the attitude of her friend who persists in wanting to conform to the rules of propriety.

She is astonished to see her friend so calm in the middle of the noises and the impatience.

Rue soufflot : Myriam, in a last effort, tries to establish a discussion.

Arthur seems impervious to the desiderata of his companion.

- " ***Then, what do we make together?*** " she asked him by sighing.

- " ***We are together, isn't it the main thing?*** "

- " ***No, you are mistaken, we are not together, we live together.*** "

- " ***You want to do semantics?*** "

What do you want to hear that I haven't told you ?

*- "**Oh no! Far be it from me, Professor! I won't be able to compete with you, but I would like you to hear me, to understand how much I suffer, how unhappy I am.** "*

What do you want to hear that I haven't told you ?

19

 The day after this last attempt at discussion, Myriam went to church to meditate, a bit like when one comes home after having tasted the horrors of life, to try to regain a little strength and a little hope.

 She is not a practicing Christian, but she believes in God. She believes in this force that is above all forces and that is able to move mountains.

But, she thought, where is this God who saw her struggling in her new life after having suffered horribly, without intervening and helping her out of this situation?

Where is he?

Where is he?

she asks herself, crying.

She wants to scream in this church in which her cry would have had a particular resonance because, it is indeed in this church that, Arthur and her stopped at the very beginning of their relationship, at the request of Myriam, to present each other holding hands before the Lord to obtain his blessing, while waiting to officialize their union by marriage.

She could not give herself to him without having made this gesture, a little to legitimize this union in which everything that will be done or will be undertaken, will necessarily be sanctified.

She is convinced of this.

She does not see things otherwise.

Arthur has been baptized, but does not practice his religion as a Christian. He doesn't know any prayers. He never sets foot in a church, not even for his father's funeral. But, for her, *(moved by he doesn't know what force)*, he made this step without thinking, entering with her in this church to obtain God's blessing. What he had not done with his two ex-wives.

It was obvious to him.

He believed in this union.

He instigated it.

He made his demand. Myriam followed him in this process, voluntarily and in all confidence.

Then, she spent time with her friend Bintou who accepted to see her, after having decided to withdraw herself from the affair.

What do you want to hear that I haven't told you ?

Stormy discussion around the decision of Myriam to leave Arthur.

Bintou is furious.

She does not understand the behavior of her friend. She ends up believing that she would be reached by a supposed curse.

She suggested that she wait a little while to ask her sister who had stayed in the village to send her some plants reputed to drive away curses.

Thus rid of this curse, she will be able to obtain all that she will want with Arthur.

It's a waste of time.

Myriam made her decision.

She obtained permission to return to her home when she had left Arthur.

Then, she returned to the apartment.

What do you want to hear that I haven't told you ?

20

A few days later, she prepared lunch as usual, then ordered a cab for later in the afternoon.

During lunch, she tries a final discussion.

For the umpteenth time, she hit a wall.

A small opening would have allowed her to cancel the cab. But .... .

What do you want to hear that I haven't told you ?

Then, that day, with a heavy heart, she announces to him that she is going to leave him.

Arthur seems not to perceive the true reasons of the decision of Myriam to leave him.

He knows that since a few days, the climate deteriorated considerably between his *(soon to be his ex)* companion and him.

The atmosphere had become unbearable, each one avoiding carefully the other.

Myriam had annexed the sofa of the living room for several weeks and did not support any more the least physical contact with her companion.

She covered herself completely when leaving the bathroom. It was no longer a question of the least intimacy between them.

Recently, the sorting in the wardrobe of the bedroom comes to confirm the arrival of the first drops of rain announcing the storm which begins to rumble in the sky above the street

What do you want to hear that I haven't told you ?

Soufflot.

Another sign: the suitcase and the travel bag, brought up from the cellar and dusted off, attest that something is preparing.

The only time they are together: the moments of meals.

Curiously, it is the only privilege that Myriam continues to grant to Arthur.

The meals continue to be prepared with the same love and the same attentions as in the first day of their life together.

Seen from the traditional side, it is not surprising. Meals are a moment of truce during which the weapons remain in the vestibule.

We don't eat with weapons in hand.

Thus, the only moments of communication still possible between them.

During this moment of meals, Myriam

What do you want to hear that I haven't told you ?

worrying about the taste of her dishes, whether it is good, if he wants more, with an infinite softness in her voice.

Minimal exchanges, but exchanges. It is better than nothing.

A real mystery for Arthur who appreciates in spite of everything, this face which becomes as by enchantment, soft, smiling and pleasant to look at.

He could ask for the composition of this or that dish. Myriam complied by giving him all the details on the preparation.

Ah, if the life of two people could be summed up only in the moments of meals, it would be wonderful.

Arthur would inevitably agree with this idea.

That day, far from suspecting that it would be the last one with Myriam, Arthur sat in the living room, in front of the television set broadcasting the news of midday.

What do you want to hear that I haven't told you ?

After having tidied up the kitchen and conditioned the remains of the meal, *(carefully arranged in the refrigerator)*, to be reheated for the dinner, as usual, Myriam returns to the living room, settles down on a chair and no longer in the sofa beside her companion.

She fixes him for a long time.

He does not understand.

He wonders.

Then, he dared:

- "I saw your luggage in the room. Are you going on a trip? "

- "No, I'm leaving you. I already told you."

- "You're leaving me? Really? "

- "Yes, I'm not going back on my decision. ...You chose to lose me then, you lost me. What more do you want? "

What do you want to hear that I haven't told you ?

In a flash, Arthur sees his whole life flash before his eyes.

First Mirella, then Nadine, his ex-wives who shared his life, and like Myriam today had taken the decision to leave without looking back.

It is probably not the ideal moment to analyze the situation.

However, he cannot help but wonder about this series of marital failures that have marked his life, and especially why he has not been able to learn from this inglorious past.

Why did the women who counted in his life leave him one after the other?

A curse? *(Bintou could help him to understand).*

Did he lack the ambition to build a stable and fruitful relationship?

In desperation, he tries one last request:

What do you want to hear that I haven't told you ?
© *Nathanaël AMAH , 2021 NATHAM Collection*

- *"I would like you to stay with me....Myriam, do not leave me. I care about you. "*

- *" Stay to do what ? "*

- *"Let's start again from scratch. Let's reinvent life, our life. Our story is not over. "*

- *"Do you hear what you are saying? Do you hear yourself talking? I have dedicated three beautiful years of my life to you. Have you seen what you've done with them? "*

- *"How can you say that to me after all we've been through together? "*

- *"Let's talk about what we've been through together. You wasted those three beautiful years I gave you, no marriage, no child, no home of our own. ... I waited in vain for a word from you to tell me that I was right to believe in you. ... With you, I never felt that feeling filled with freshness and honesty as a first love. ... Must I continue? "*

What do you want to hear that I haven't told you ?

- "Honey, tell me: what do you want to hear that I haven't told you? "

- "I LOVE YOU!   You have never told me that in the three years I have been with you. "

Myriam got up and left without looking back.

111

What do you want to hear that I haven't told you ?
© Nathanaël AMAH , 2021 NATHAM Collection

E N D

What do you want to hear that I haven't told you ?

What do you want to hear that I haven't told you ?

What do you want to hear that I haven't told you ?

(namah1000@gmail.com)

What do you want to hear that I haven't told you ?

Éditeur : BoD-Books on Demand, 12/14 rond point des
Champs Élysées, 75008 Paris, France
Impression: BoD-Books on Demand, Norderstedt,
Allemagne
ISBN : **9782322174317**
Dépôt légal : May, 2021

What do you want to hear that I haven't told you ?

FSC
www.fsc.org

MIXTE

Papier issu
de sources
responsables
Paper from
responsible sources

FSC® C105338